D1569302

 **BOOK REVIEWS**

Here's what people are saying:

Easy to read, with funny illustrations....
from BULLETIN OF THE CENTER FOR CHILDREN'S BOOKS

*This affectionate tale of transformation
is bursting with humor and good will....*
from PUBLISHERS WEEKLY

... fresh and wildly funny....
from BOOKLIST

Weekly Readers Books Presents

A Package for Miss Marshwater

Elfie Donnelly
pictures by Ute Krause

Dial Books for Young Readers · New York

This book is a presentation of Weekly Reader Books.
Weekly Reader Books offers book clubs for children
from preschool through high school. For further
information write to: **Weekly Reader Books,**
4343 Equity Drive, Columbus, Ohio 43228.

Published by arrangement with
Dial Books for Young Readers,
A Division of NAL Penguin Inc.
Weekly Reader is a trademark of Field Publications.

First published in the United States 1987
by Dial Books for Young Readers
A Division of NAL Penguin Inc.
2 Park Avenue
New York, New York 10016

Published simultaneously in Canada
by Fitzhenry & Whiteside Limited, Toronto
First published in German in 1986
as *Ein Paket für Frau Löbenzahn*
by Otto Maier Verlag Ravensburg
Copyright © 1986 by Otto Maier Verlag Ravensburg
Translated by Lenny Hort
American text copyright © 1987 by
Dial Books for Young Readers
Typography by Beth Peck
All rights reserved
Printed in U.S.A.
First Edition
W
1 3 5 7 9 10 8 6 4 2

Library of Congress Cataloging in Publication Data
Donnelly, Elfie. A package for Miss Marshwater.
Summary: Miss Marshwater's life is changed for the
better by the arrival of two talking platypuses.
[1. Platypus—Fiction.] I. Krause, Ute, ill. II. Title.
PZ7.D7193Pac 1987 [E] 87-5257
ISBN 0-8037-0453-4
ISBN 0-8037-0454-2 (lib. bdg.)

Miss Marshwater was a lady.

She drank her tea from fine bone china. She'd raise the cup ever so carefully. The little finger of her right hand always pointed off to one side. She never slurped.

Miss Marshwater always wore elegant shoes. Even when they pinched her toes, she never complained. She wouldn't dream of cursing. No, that's not true. She certainly dreamed about it. But a lady would never do such a thing!

Miss Marshwater always carried her fine alligator handbag when she went out. She wore white gloves and a hat on her head. And she tripped along daintily.

Strictly speaking, Miss Marshwater was not completely happy being a lady. It was so much trouble. In fact, it was tedious. Miss Marshwater used to be the wildest little girl on her block. If she wasn't pulling another girl's hair or copying somebody's homework, she was fighting with Paul, the baker's son, or sticking gum on the teacher's chair. Time after time her mother said, "You'll never get to be a lady that way!"

Little Emmie Marshwater must have heard that ten times a day. It shot in one ear and out the other. But somehow it

must have sunk in. Young Miss Marshwater resolved to become a lady. She learned to knit and make polite conversation and even learned to play the piano. Because Mother had told her that *any* proper lady could play the piano.

Early one morning Miss Marshwater was practicing a piece by Bach on the harpsichord. (A harpsichord looks like a piano, but it sounds sweeter and more ladylike.) Miss Marshwater couldn't quite get the melody right. She tried over and over and over. So it was no wonder when old Mrs. Wolfbottom from downstairs banged a broomstick on the ceiling. Miss Marshwater stopped playing right then. She sighed. She slammed the lid of her beautiful ladylike harpsichord.

Then she heard the buzzer ringing. Miss Marshwater made a face and held her ears. (Ladies' ears are so sensitive to noise.) She stumbled for the door. Those stupid high-heeled shoes!

That had to be Mrs. Wolfbottom coming to complain about the music.

But it wasn't shriveled old Mrs. Wolfbottom at the door. This man was huge, and stocky as an elephant, in a blue uniform. There was an emblem on his sleeve. "Are you Miss Marshwater?" he asked, and then pressed an enormous package into her arms. She teetered under the weight of the load. "Unusual name you got, isn't it? So long!"

He was gone. Miss Marshwater looked
pretty confused. Ladies are supposed to get
perfumed letters, she thought, not unwieldy
packages from great big mailmen.

Panting, she dragged the package to the
table by the harpsichord. She read the return
address: *Everett Marshwater, 1 Elm St., Sydney,
Australia.* Cousin Everett! Miss Marshwater
wiped a tear. She was so touched that he had
thought of her, she forgot for a minute that
she'd never much cared for him.

Could he have remembered her birthday?
It was only a week away. Miss Marshwater
carefully tugged at the tight string around the
package. It was hard to open. "All of these
awful knots," she said. The sound of her own
voice startled her. She didn't hear it very
often when she was home all alone. And she
was always home alone. But then she didn't
usually talk to herself.

Inside the big box was another box. There
was another box inside that one. And then
another. And another.

By the time Miss Marshwater
was down to the last box,
she was sweating more like
a track star than a lady.

"Merciful God in heaven"
slipped out of her.

She clapped a shocked hand
over her mouth. Who was swearing like that?
Surely not herself! Miss Marshwater glanced
cautiously over her shoulder and looked
around the room. She peered into every nook
and corner. She was all alone—or was she?

Suddenly she heard a gentle scratching

noise. Mice! thought a
fearful Miss Marshwater.
Ladies are terrified of
mice. She held her ear
to the little carton.

No doubt about it.
The scratching noise was

coming from inside. Miss Marshwater broke
into another sweat. Now it was from fear even
more than the strain of opening the package.
She rummaged feverishly through her sewing
basket, looking for her scissors. There they
were! Emmie Marshwater anxiously ripped
through layers of masking tape and tossed
them carelessly on the floor.

Wood shavings popped out at her. Miss
Marshwater held her breath. She was terrified.
Maybe something strange was in that package.
Maybe something wicked.

Just then she noticed that every one of the cardboard boxes was covered with little air holes.

"Plotch" went the first something. And the second something went "Plotch."

Miss Emmie Marshwater closed her eyes and counted to one hundred. It was an old trick of her mother's, and it was always good at scary moments.

And then she heard light breathing. Very, very cautiously she opened her left eye just a crack. She peeped out her right eye, then shut both eyes tight. Surely she was dreaming.

"Merciful God in heaven," said a voice.

"Merciful God in heaven," said another voice.

Two gray animals were sitting on Miss Marshwater's shiny parquet floor. They were the strangest animals she had ever seen. They sat up and looked at Miss Marshwater with big eyes. "Merciful God in heaven," said the first animal. "Merciful God in heaven," said the second.

"Please stay where you are!" begged Miss Marshwater. She was worried that they might jump on her lap. Then she would surely die of fright. Or faint at least. Without taking her eyes off the creatures—

who, on top of everything else, had wide bills like ducks and flat, brown beaverlike tails— Miss Marshwater went rummaging through the carton. "Ah, here it is." Finally she found a letter from cousin Everett.

The page trembled in Miss Marshwater's hand. And it wasn't easy to read with one eye on the creatures.

Dear Emmie, All best wishes for your birthday. I'm sending you two pets I raised

so you won't be so
lonely. The one
with the red spot
on his bill is called
A, and the other
one is Bea. (Bea is
a girl.) They are

platypuses. Bea lays an egg every now and
then, so don't panic if she does. But please
don't eat it. They are housebroken and easy
to take care of, and they eat anything you eat.
They're very sweet. They don't know how to

speak on their own,
but they will repeat
anything you say.

Miss Marshwater put
the letter down. She
couldn't believe it.
She read the last line
out loud.

"They will repeat anything you say."

"Say," said A.

"Say," said Bea.

Then the room was quiet. Miss Marshwater sighed. Then A sighed. Bea sighed. "Go jump in a lake," said Miss Marshwater, forgetting that she was a lady.

"Jump in a lake," said A.

"Lake," said Bea. She cackled.

"No cackling in here!" shouted an indignant Miss Marshwater.

"Here," said A. Bea was silent. Emmie Marshwater felt her knees knocking.

She stood up wearily and smoothed out
her skirt. The platypuses stood up too. They
waddled after Miss Marshwater on their hind
legs. They had webbed feet. And they stood
pretty tall. They came up past Miss Marshwater's knees. She went into the kitchen.

"I just won't pay attention," muttered Miss
Marshwater.

"Won't pay attention," said A.

"Attention," muttered Bea.

Miss Marshwater gritted her teeth.

A and Bea gazed intently at their new
mistress through the kitchen doorway. She
was getting herself a banana. Slowly she
peeled it. This is not happening, she thought.
I'll just eat my banana, and when I turn
around, those monsters will have vanished.
Miss Marshwater chewed slowly. She
swallowed. Then she turned around.

Where were A and Bea? Still right there in

the doorway. A's little front paws were folded over his chest. One of his hind paws was tapping on the floor. Bea lay on her chest with her head propped on a front paw.

Miss Marshwater felt her throat tighten. She threw the banana peel on the floor. "Hee hee," went Bea. A gave Miss Emmie Marshwater a dirty look. He picked up the banana peel and tossed it in the garbage pail. Miss Marshwater was turning red. She was so ashamed. A lady would *never* throw her banana peel on the floor. Why, any decent platypus would throw it in the trash.

Miss Marshwater was in a daze. More than anything she wanted to put the animals back in their box and mark it *Return to Australia. With Deepest Thanks.* But she didn't. She was too scared to pick them up. Their fur *was* rather pretty. But they might bite. Or maybe nip a finger—or something else. She walked cautiously out of the kitchen. She hoped A and Bea would stay where they were. "Don't stare at me like that!" shouted Miss Marshwater.

"Don't stare at me like that!" roared A.

"Me like that! Hee hee!" giggled Bea.

Miss Marshwater slammed the door shut and locked it. She rushed to her armchair and flopped down. At last it was quiet again.

Miss Emmie Marshwater began to cry. She hadn't done that for years. But it was so easy to sit down and howl. What a life! A runny nose, shoes that hurt, and two platypuses locked in the kitchen. Poor sad Miss Emmie Marshwater felt very sorry for herself. She pulled out her delicate lace handkerchief and blew her nose.

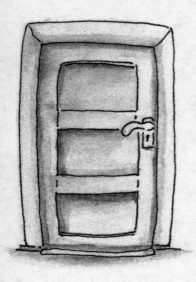

After a while the tears stopped. She was all cried out. Then she heard a funny noise in the kitchen. A noise like a frying pan sizzling. Now what? All she could do for the last five minutes was stare at the telephone. If she could just think of someone to call for help. Her two best friends were on vacation. Her sister? No, she didn't want to call her. They were sure to argue. Why, Miss Marshwater's sister, Ellie, wasn't one bit a lady. She made a joke out of everything. And she always wore sneakers and blue jeans. She had nothing at all in common with Emmie.

What if she called the zoo? She looked up the number in the phone book and dialed.

"Hello? I have two
platypuses right here
and I need to—"

"Platypuses are found
only in Australia,
ma'am," said the man
on the phone.

"They were sent to me, and I can't stand
the way they always repeat everything I
say." Emmie Marshwater whimpered and
started to cry again.

"They repeat everything you say?" the
man asked slowly.

"Yes!" Emmie sniffled.
"And they keep giving
me these dirty looks!"
There was a pause.
Then there was a click.
The man had hung up.

Miss Marshwater stared at the phone in disbelief. "He thought I was crazy," she said to herself. She giggled nervously. Anybody would think she was crazy after hearing that story. But maybe . . . maybe she really *was* crazy! She had to be. She had only imagined those platypuses.

They didn't really exist. Miss Marshwater looked at the boxes. If that were true, what really was in her package?

No. There was no such thing as a talking platypus. It was just her crazy imagination. Definitely. No doubt about it. Miss Marshwater went straight over and opened the kitchen door and—

A and Bea were seated on chairs at the table. Each one of them had a plate and silverware. On each plate was a fried egg with a dab of catsup in the middle and garnished with parsley.

A third place had been set. Miss Marshwater sat down unsteadily. A jumped up and ran to the stove. He got the frying pan and served her an egg.

"No, thank you, no catsup," she said wearily. Bea nimbly screwed the cap back on the bottle. *"Bon appétit,"* said Miss Emmie Marshwater.

"Bon appétit," said A.

"Appétit," said Bea.

"Bon appétit," said A, and passed Bea the pepper.

"*Bon appétit*," Bea repeated politely. She stuck her bill in the egg and slurped it right up. She wiped herself clean with a paper towel.

"Tsk, tsk," went A. He took knife and fork in his front paws and ate very slowly and carefully. Almost like a lady, Miss Marshwater thought. Like a little gentleman. She stared at her egg. She must be the first person ever to have a platypus fry an egg for her. And Emmie couldn't help noticing that it didn't taste bad at all.

Bea got up and walked to the bathroom. All by herself. She pulled the chain down. A moment later Miss Marshwater heard the toilet flush.

"Housebroken!" Miss Marshwater exclaimed from the kitchen. An animal surely couldn't be any more housebroken than that.

"Housebroken!" A said proudly. He picked up the dishes and washed them in the sink. Miss Marshwater had to sit down. Suddenly she felt very woozy, as if she'd had too much to drink. That had only happened once— at her sister's wedding, many years ago. She could barely remember it now.

Strawberry cooler. Yes, it was the strawberry cooler. After a few glasses Miss Emmie Marshwater had started to giggle and say strawberry fooler. Or crawberry muler. Or strawbeetle cooler. Beetle juice. Strongberry cooler. Wrongberry cooler.

"Rawberry drooler," Miss Marshwater said, giggling in the kitchen.

"Rawberry drooler," said A.

"Rawberry drooler?" asked Bea, who had returned from the bathroom and was washing her paws.

"Strawberry cooler," Miss Marshwater corrected. Then A went to the refrigerator and pulled out every beverage he could find. But Miss Marshwater was smiling. These platypuses certainly aimed to please.

"Strawberry cooler," she finally nodded.

"Hee," giggled A.

"Hee hee hee," giggled Bea. But when A gave her a look, she quieted down.

All at once Miss Marshwater was feeling fine. There wasn't even the tiniest bit of fear left in her. She was so happy that she scampered into the living room and sat down at the harpsichord.

Her toes were cold. Goodness, she was barefoot! So unladylike. With Bea on her right and A on her left, she shrugged her shoulders and began to play. No doubt about it; Miss Marshwater wasn't acting like herself at all.

The two platypuses watched wide-eyed as Miss Marshwater's fingers moved up and down the keys. Bea was excited. Cautiously she pressed a paw on a key. She shrunk back when it actually produced a note.

Miss Marshwater got up and fetched two stools. A and Bea understood at once and sat themselves down.

"*Bourrée*, by Bach," Emmie Marshwater announced.

"Puree!" said Bea, looking hungry.

"*Bourrée!*" corrected A.

Bea turned away, looking insulted.

Miss Marshwater played with gusto. A and Bea swayed back and forth.

"You never heard real music at Cousin Everett's, did you?" Miss Marshwater said when she was finished playing, although she was quite sure they hadn't. "He probably made you listen to jazz." Jazz always made her shudder; it was so wild and unladylike.

A and Bea jumped on Miss Marshwater and started banging wildly at the keyboard like jazz musicians. She clapped her hands over her ears. "Hey!" Miss Marshwater held her breath. Bea's fat little bottom was bouncing all over Emmie Marshwater's lap. "No, no, no!" she yelled. She grabbed A and sat him back down on his stool.

Then she grabbed Bea and sat her on the other one.

"A harpsichord must be treated with love," she said.

"With love!" said A.

"With loooovvve!" Bea said sweetly. And Miss Marshwater was amazed at how much she already cared for Bea.

"I'm Emmie," she said suddenly.

"Emmie!" said A. "Emmie!"

"Emmmmmie!" whispered Bea.

"A!" said A and pointed to himself. "Bea!" and he pointed at Bea.

"Bea!" said Bea. "A!" she giggled at A. "Emmie!" She nudged Emmie Marshwater on the shoulder with her bill.

All at once Miss Marshwater felt that she wasn't alone anymore. Maybe they could both really love her, even if no one else did. Their gray platypus fur felt so soft and cuddly. Maybe it would even be all right to let A and Bea sleep in her bed.

"Just like my old teddy bear," she said out loud, and smiled.

"Teddy bear!" said Bea, and cuddled against Emmie.

"Like my old teddy bear!" A dug his head into Emmie Marshwater's lap.

It was dark now. She had played the harpsichord all afternoon long, and A and Bea were getting tired. Emmie yawned.

A yawned. And Bea yawned.

Miss Marshwater closed the lid over the keyboard. "Bedtime," she said.

"Bedtime!" said A.

"Bedtime." Bea yawned again.

Emmie decided that she would sleep better without her pets. She pulled some blankets out of the closet and made up a little bed for A and Bea.

Why did Bea look so sad when Emmie said "Good night" and shut the bedroom door?

"Good night," said A.

"Night," said Bea, and waved.

Miss Marshwater slept very well that night. Much better than usual. For the first time in many years she was not alone. She felt like part of a family.

Miss Marshwater woke up in a good mood.
Much, much better than usual. A and Bea
were sleeping beside her. Bea's bill was open
a crack. And A was snoring lightly.

"You naughty boy," Emmie Marshwater
said softly, and got out of bed.

"Naughty boy," Bea muttered in her sleep,
and turned over on her side.

Miss Marshwater went to the tub and took
a long hot shower. She sang "The Little Old
Lady From Pasadena" and thought about
what to make the three of them for breakfast.

But there was a surprise in the kitchen.
Bea was taking a bubble bath in the sink.
"Lalalala . . . naughty boy . . . merciful God
in heaven . . ." she sang. Miss Marshwater
just laughed.

A had already gotten breakfast on the table. Toast popped out of the toaster, the egg timer was ringing, and the coffee was perking. Bea got out of the sink and shook herself.

"Tsk, tsk," went A. Bea hurried off to the bathroom to dry herself. She got tangled in a white towel and came back looking like a little duck-billed ghost. Emmie laughed and helped unwrap her. "Say thank you," said Emmie.

"Say thank you," said Bea.

"Say thank you," said A.

"Say thank you," said Bea again.

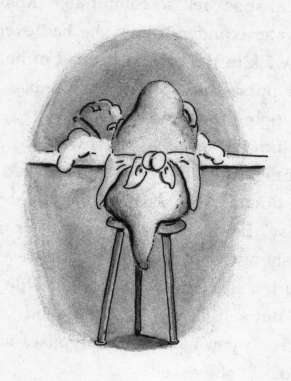

They ate breakfast together. A did the
dishes, and then Miss Marshwater went shopping. It was an easy walk for a change because
she was wearing different shoes.

Her ladylike high-heeled shoes had simply
vanished so she had to put on flat ones.

The flat shoes felt so comfortable, Miss Marshwater wondered how she had ever been able to walk in the others. Instead of her fine alligator purse she took a large tote bag. She was shopping for three now.

"Good morning, Miss Marshwater," said Mr. Baumgartner, the grocer. He looked her up and down. What was so different about her today? Emmie Marshwater ran her fingers nervously over her head. She hadn't even combed her hair and was feeling a little messy. But she liked it. She felt good.

"What do you have that platypuses would really love?" she asked.

Now he was sure there was something odd about her today. "Platypuses?" he asked her.

"Platypuses," Miss Marshwater repeated.

"I don't know," said Mr. Baumgartner. "We have some delicious treats pussycats meow for."

"Aren't platypuses Australian?" asked a boy holding a bag of potatoes.

"Well, Australians love cookouts, don't they?" Mr. Baumgartner said. "And aren't they crazy about baked beans?"

"Not Cousin Everett," she said absent-mindedly as she looked in the fruit aisle. What would make A and Bea really happy?

"Kiwi fruits are from Australia," the boy said, pointing to a small round brown fruit that was new to Miss Marshwater.

"Okay, then, two pounds of kiwis, if they're

fresh," said Emmie Marshwater. Mr. Baumgartner, quite surprised, wrapped them up.
For years Miss Marshwater had come in every
morning and never gotten more than a roll, a
pint of milk, a yogurt, and maybe a couple of
oranges. But today she wanted kiwis!

"Very good. And your milk?"

"Yes, thank you, half a gallon please."
And to Mr. Baumgartner's amazement she
also bought a dozen eggs, a family-size
package of muffins, and a good deal more.

Miss Marshwater skipped home, glad to be wearing comfortable shoes because her shopping bag was *so* heavy today. She panted up the stairs. Mrs. Wolfbottom was blocking the door. "It's a disgrace," she yelled, "it's an absolute disgrace. All morning long, that racket. Can't you take up another instrument? The kazoo, maybe?"

"I haven't even been home," Miss Marshwater yelled back, "and I've had it up to here with you and your complaints!"

Mrs. Wolfbottom gasped. "How can you talk like that to a lady!"

Miss Marshwater was ready to spit.

"I'll play my harp-sichord whenever I feel like it, all right! And I'll talk to you any way I want to, all right! And I'll— I'll—" But Mrs. Wolfbottom finally turned around and stalked away very indignantly. Miss Marshwater felt like she was walking on air. She'd been wanting to tell Mrs. Wolfbottom off for years.

And now she'd done it. And high time too. All right!

She opened the door. "Guess what I have, children," she called out. She meant A and Bea, of course. But they were nowhere to be seen.

"A!" she called, "Bea!" For a minute she thought they were gone, and she felt very sad. Just then a single note came from the harpsichord. And then one note more. And then another. That could only mean . . .

She looked in the living room. A cleared his throat. Bea giggled. They were sitting together at the harpsichord.

"*Bourrée* by Bach," said A, and placed his front paws on the keys.

"Puree by Bach," said Bea.

They started to play. Very slowly at first, then faster. They played the entire piece exactly as she had played it for them. From first note to last without a single mistake.

Miss Marshwater listened in wide-eyed, open-mouthed astonishment. These little platypuses were amazing! What other fantastic things could they do? When the piece was over, Miss Emmie Marshwater clapped like a thunderstorm. "Bravo!" she shouted over and over. "Brav-o!"

"Bravo," cried Bea, and clapped her paws. "Bravo," said A as he applauded himself.

Miss Marshwater was so busy clapping that she dropped her shopping bag. The kiwis rolled by the harpsichord.

"Kiwis! Kiwis!" Bea clicked her bill with excitement and chased after them. She sat on her bottom and stuffed one fruit after another down her bill.

"Kiwis!" cried A. "Everett kiwis!"

Miss Marshwater flopped on the floor. Most unladylike. She watched them wolf

down the kiwis and then carefully bit into one herself. It wasn't bad at all if you peeled it first.

So they could say "kiwis" without having it said to them first. And also "Everett." Maybe the two of them could really learn how to converse, like good little children. Like human children. For the first time in her life Emmie Marshwater was feeling like she belonged.

The doorbell rang. It was Mrs. Wolfbottom again. "That noise is unbearable, Miss Marshwater! I really must protest," she scolded.

A and Bea giggled. "Protest!" they said.

Mrs. Wolfbottom stared at A and Bea. "There are no dogs allowed here. And no ducks. No—whatever you call them. Do you have a license for those animals? I'm telling the landlord that you're keeping duck-dogs, or giant hamsters, or—what sort of creature is that anyway?"

"A," said A.

"Bea," said Bea.

"I'd like you to meet A and Bea," Miss Marshwater said, with a hand on her mouth to keep from laughing.

"It's not funny!" screamed Mrs. Wolfbottom, who was turning red.

"Not funny!" A and B said at once, giggling loudly.

Mrs. Wolfbottom marched back downstairs, holding her head.

A and Bea started wrestling each other on the rug. They looked so funny together that Miss Marshwater wanted to roll around with them.

"Emmie, Emmie!" A cried, and pulled Miss Emmie Marshwater onto the rug.

"Emmie, Emmie!" Bea climbed up on Emmie's side and tickled her.

And downstairs poor Mrs. Wolfbottom banged her broomstick on the ceiling.

After lunch—A made home fries and Bea made a tossed salad—they played six-handed sonatas till it got dark.

It went on that way with A and Bea and Miss Marshwater—who wasn't the least bit ladylike anymore. She tossed her purse in the trash, along with her proper hat and white gloves. She was too happy to bother looking for her pointy shoes. All three of them had a marvelous time laughing, singing, and playing together. And dear Mrs. Wolfbottom didn't get any sleep at all.

Then a few weeks later A woke Emmie up in the middle of the night. "It's dark, A," Emmie murmured, "let me sleep." But A kept at it. He started jumping up and down on the bed.

"Bea, Bea," he kept shouting.

Emmie groggily turned the light on. Was everything all right? She found Bea under the bed alongside two eggs. But they didn't look like ordinary eggs. And they weren't. They were platypus eggs. And they were moving. Emmie's eyes popped open. "Bea," Emmie Marshwater shouted, "Bea! Don't tell me we're having babies!" But inside she was very, very pleased.

"Babies," Bea said with a nod, "babies!"
"Babies, babies!" A started to dance.

An hour passed. Then two. Emmie could barely stay awake. Then before her eyes one egg hatched, and then the other.

Two tiny round little bills poked out, and two tiny rumpled little creatures crawled out in the open air, shook themselves all over, and snuggled up to Bea's belly.

"Boy, oh boy," Emmie cried as she wiped a tear of joy.

"Boyoboy!"
said Bea.

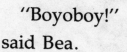

"Boyoboyoboy!" cried A.
"Boyoboy," a little one
peeped.
"Boyoboy," the other
one peeped.

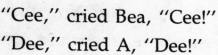

"Cee," cried Bea, "Cee!"
"Dee," cried A, "Dee!"

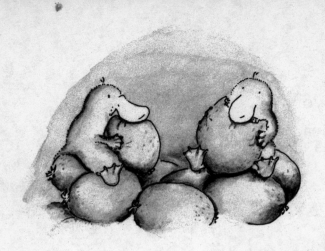

And so it went. The babies were named
Cee and Dee. They always repeated anything
you said, and they loved to tussle on the rug,
eat kiwis, and practice on the harpsichord.
Mrs. Wolfbottom reported it all to the landlord. Then she followed the landlord's advice
and moved away to a warmer, more restful
climate.

And Emmie Marshwater? Now that she
wasn't a lady anymore, she could dress any
way she wanted and frolic on the floor with
her duck-billed friends. Or she could sit at
the keyboard with A, Bea, Cee, and Dee.

"*Bourrée* by Bach," said A.

"Puree my Bach," said Bea.

"Poolay Bach," said Cee, but after all, he was only a baby.

"Lullalock," said Dee. She still had trouble saying her *P*'s.

And they all lived happily ever after.

Even Mr. Baumgartner, the grocer. He sold
a fortune in kiwi fruit to Emmie Marshwater.
He didn't mind one bit that she wasn't a lady
anymore. Now she was simply a woman.
Just plain Emmie Marshwater.

And *that's* the story.